ROBIN HOOD

Editor: Heather Hammond
Cover Illustration: Terry Riley
Illustrations: Terry Riley
Typesetting: Midland Typesetters

Robin Hood
First published in 2007 by
Budget Books Pty Ltd
45–55 Fairchild Street
Heatherton Victoria 3202 Australia

10 9 8 7 6 5 4 3 2
12 11 10 09 08

ISBN: 978 1 7418 1484 2

Printed & bound in India

Some of the characters you'll meet in this story:

Robin Hood – a courageous young man who is out-lawed and sentenced to death after being cruelly tricked by the Sheriff of Nottingham's men

Little John – Robin's close friend and right-hand man

Allan a Dale – the outlaw minstrel who sings for Robin and his men

Will Stutely – one of the first to join Robin in Sherwood Forest

Will Scarlet – a trusty member of the band of outlaws, and one of the few men strong enough to beat Robin in battle

Friar Tuck – the portly and jolly friar with a taste for the good things in life

Midge – the miller who taught Robin a painful lesson and then joined him in Sherwood Forest

Tim the Tanner – the man who gave Little John a bloody nose

Maid Marian – Robin's sweetheart

The Sheriff of Nottingham, **Prince John** and **Sir Guy of Gisborne** – Robin's sworn enemies

Contents

Introduction
The Legend of Robin Hood

The legend of Robin Hood, England's most daring and loved outlaw, emerged from the mists of history almost eight hundred years ago. Stories about Robin first appeared in ancient ballads and poems. They told how Robin and his Merry Men of Sherwood Forest fought for justice against tyrants, and stole from the rich to help the poor.

The legends brought to life Robin's sweetheart, Maid Marian, and his band of fellow outlaws. They included such fearless men of honor as the gentle giant Little John, noble Will Scarlet, the ballad singer Allan a Dale, Midge the miller and jovial Friar Tuck.

But Robin had three all-powerful enemies; the cruel and greedy Sheriff of Nottingham, his right-hand man, Sir Guy of Gisborne, and Prince John, the treacherous brother of King Richard the Lionheart.

Robin Hood

Only Robin and his courageous band stood between those three traitors and a cunning plot to steal the throne of England!

Chapter 1
Outlaw!

The arrow from young Robin Hood's bow arched high into the blue sky above Sherwood Forest. At last, it began to slow and sink towards the ground again.

The fate of that one arrow would change Robin's life forever and launch one of old England's most famous legends.

That sunny morning in the ancient forest, Robin had been walking hand-in-hand with Maid Marian, his childhood sweetheart. A happier couple you could not have found in all England.

Spring had sprung and bursting buds had turned the winter forest into a wild world of the greenwood. Birds sang joyously from every tree. The royal deer were grazing on the new season's lush grass.

Robin, just nineteen years old, and Marian, two years younger, were laughing and talking together as they walked happily back towards the small village of Loxley, where they lived.

They spotted four men beside the track. Robin recognized them as the Sheriff of Nottingham's foresters. Their job was to patrol the forest, making sure no one stole any of the King's deer. These men were enjoying a breakfast of bread and cheese.

Robin knew it was dangerous to meddle with the Sheriff's men. The Sheriff had become a powerful man since King Richard the Lionheart had gone away to fight in the Holy Wars. Now he supported Richard's treacherous brother, Prince John, a man who wanted the throne of England for himself.

Robin and Marian simply wished the men a good day and passed on by. But the Sheriff's men were in good spirits and thought they would have some sport with the couple.

"You're not old enough to carry a weapon like that," laughed one of the foresters, pointing to the great bow around Robin's shoulders and the quiver of arrows dangling at his waist. "You're but a child."

Robin, a spirited, hot-blooded youth, should have ignored the remark. But his pride was hurt. "I'm a better archer than you'll ever be!" he snapped angrily.

"What's your name, boy?" asked one of the

Outlaw!

Walking in the forest

men, starting to laugh at him. "You'd be better off at home, drinking your mother's milk!"

Robin's blood boiled at the rudeness of the man. "I'm Robin of Loxley and I'll bet I can shoot a better arrow than any of you," he replied boldly.

"That's a boast that could cost you your life," said the man, looking around for a target.

He spotted a deer with fierce, proud antlers, grazing in the far distance. Now he set a terrible trap for Robin.

"See that large deer," he said, with a sneering smile. "I'll bet you a gold coin that you couldn't bring it down with a single arrow."

Robin knew that all the deer in Sherwood belonged to the King. He also knew that to kill or steal one was a crime that a man could be hanged for. Yet his youthful pride and anger blinded him to the dangers.

Robin reached for his bow, a beautiful home-made weapon of the finest yew wood. Then he took an arrow from his quiver and notched it onto the bow string.

Raising the bow with his left hand, he took aim and pulled back the bowstring until it touched his ear.

"No, Robin!" cried Marian suddenly. "You

Outlaw!

Robin took aim.

mustn't do it. It's a trap. They'll hang you!"

Robin hesitated for a moment, but then another of the foresters insulted him again.

"Oh, so you're going to listen to a silly little girl, are you?" said the man. "Do you always hide behind her skirts?"

Robin was furious. Before he knew it, he had released the bowstring.

"Twang!" The arrow sped on its way, high into the sky. Robin's aim was true. When the arrow whistled to earth again it struck the deer a deadly blow.

"Ha!" cried Robin. "What do you think of that for a shot? The gold coin is mine!"

"That shot will cost you more than a gold coin," laughed the forester. "When the Sheriff hears you've killed one of the King's deer, there will be a price on your head!"

"But you made a bet," said Robin. "You owe me a gold coin."

"I owe you nothing!" roared the man. "You were fool enough to shoot at the King's deer. So you will pay – probably with your life!"

"Arrest him!" ordered another of the men.

Robin shouted at Marian, telling her to run home. Then he darted into the forest.

The Sheriff's men gave chase, shooting

several arrows at him. It was an arrow whistling past his head that forced Robin to turn and shoot back in self defense. He took careful aim. Robin didn't want to hit one of the Sheriff's men. He only wanted to frighten them off.

But just as he released the arrow, he lost his footing in the grass. The arrow struck one of his pursuers squarely in the chest, killing him instantly.

Now Robin was truly running for his life. Not only had he killed one of the King's deer, he had also killed one of the Sheriff's foresters.

Robin's life would never be the same again.

He was now an outlaw.

Chapter 2
The Great Oak Tree

Robin ran until he was nearly exhausted. The Sheriff's men had long given up the chase. Sherwood Forest covered a huge area of more than one hundred thousand acres. It could be a frightening place. Few travelers dared to enter it because it was known to be a hiding place for outlaws.

In summer, the greenwood hung thickly over the tracks that criss-crossed the forest. Any traveler who was bold enough to enter the forest could see no more than a few yards in front of him.

Robin, however, knew the forest very well. It was his childhood playground. He knew its tracks and ways better than any man, and knew exactly where he was going.

That morning, Robin headed for the safest place he could think of. Right in the middle of the forest stood a gigantic oak tree. He had sought shelter in it as a child during games of

Robin headed for the safest place he could think of.

hide-and-seek. He knew that the Sheriff of Nottingham's men would never find him there.

Robin reached the Great Oak by evening. At last, he felt happier. The tree was like an old friend to him. He climbed up and slipped into a deep bed of leaves, formed where three large branches joined the tree trunk. It was as comfortable as any feather bed.

Robin felt tired and lonely as he watched the last light of the day disappear.

"I cannot change what has happened," he thought sadly, as squirrels played in the boughs above him. "What is done is done. I killed in anger and youthful temper. Now I must pay the price."

He knew he could no longer return home to his village. As he slipped into a troubled sleep that evening, his last thoughts were of Marian. He was missing her already.

***

Even as Robin fell asleep, the Sheriff of Nottingham was deciding his fate.

The foresters had returned to Nottingham Castle and reported what Robin had done. They made no mention of why he had shot a deer.

The Sheriff was wearing a purple robe and cap, a great gold chain of office around his neck and a shining broadsword at his waist. He was having a supper of roasted venison, lamb chops, roast beef, pig's trotters and a mountain of different vegetables. He didn't like being disturbed while eating.

"Hang the man!" he ordered, stuffing another piece of venison into his mouth and rubbing his great fat stomach.

"He escaped us," said one of the soldiers nervously.

"Then go and find him," snarled the Sheriff. "Bring him back in irons and hang him. Now leave me in peace to eat my supper!"

"He vanished into Sherwood Forest," said the second soldier rather quietly.

The Sheriff knew full well the dangers of going into Sherwood Forest after outlaws. He was frightened of setting foot in the place. Half a dozen outlaws hidden in the greenwood could outwit a small army of soldiers.

"Right!" he said, losing his patience. "Put a reward of two hundred pounds on the lad's head, dead or alive. Some peasant will bring him to us for the money. But I'd prefer him taken alive so I can hang him from the battlements as

"Hang the man!"

a lesson to others. Now get out of my sight! My meat is getting cold."

The next morning, the Sheriff's men nailed notices to trees along the tracks leading into Sherwood Forest. It wasn't long before Robin found one. He read it:

Wanted
Robin Hood of Loxley
For murder of a Sheriff's man
and killing one of the King's deer.
Reward £200

Chapter 3
A Lonely Home in Sherwood Forest

Robin laid low in Sherwood Forest for the next few months, hardly ever straying far from the Great Oak. Only once did he see a party of the Sheriff of Nottingham's soldiers searching for him. From the safety of his tree, he watched them pass below him. The Sheriff's men never found a trace of him.

Marian, of course, knew his hiding place. She had played in the woods with him as a child and guessed where he would be. In the months ahead, she brought him bread and cheese when she could.

But Marian soon had to stop seeing Robin. The Sheriff discovered that she was Robin's sweetheart and his soldiers began to follow her everywhere, in case she should lead them to Robin.

Even without Marian's help, Robin ate well in the forest. He knew he might as well be

A Lonely Home in Sherwood Forest

He watched them pass below him.

for killing one deer as three. So whenever his larder was empty, he killed another deer for food. He was never short of water, either. There was a small stream of clear, ice-cool water flowing beside his leafy home.

Robin wasn't completely alone. He knew there were other outlaws in the forest; people escaping the Sheriff's cruel and unfair justice. It wasn't long before he met one of them.

Robin had set off one morning to explore some of his childhood haunts in the forest. He hadn't gone far when he had to cross a river. He knew the place well. Many years earlier a huge oak tree had fallen across the river and the trunk had made a bridge.

When Robin reached the river he found the tree bridge still there. A giant of a man was approaching it from the other side. There was only room for one to cross the river on the tree trunk.

"Stand back, lad!" shouted the stranger. "Let the better and stronger man cross first."

"In that case," said Robin boldly, "you had better let me pass first!"

"You're nothing but a child," replied the man. "Now stand aside. I don't want to have to hurt you."

If there was one thing that annoyed Robin, it was to be called a child. He took out his bow and warned the man to stand back.

"Watch out, youngster!" the big man growled. "If you shoot that arrow, I'll tan your hide until it's the color of a red squirrel! Besides only a coward would shoot a man unarmed, except for an oak staff."

Robin saw that the man's only weapon was a quarterstaff – a long, thick pole cut from a

"Stand back, lad!"

tree. He immediately put down his bow. "I'll not be called a coward," he cried, "I'll cut myself a quarterstaff to fight you fairly."

Robin disappeared into the undergrowth and returned a few moments later with a thick staff, about six feet long. The stranger was now standing on the tree trunk in the middle of the river, waiting for Robin with both hands on his quarterstaff.

Robin gripped his own staff tightly. Then he leapt onto the tree trunk and advanced . . .

Chapter 4
Little John

For a long moment, the two men stared at each other as they balanced themselves on the tree trunk. Then the stranger made the first attack, lashing out viciously with his staff. Robin was not prepared for the blow. It clipped him on the head.

"Ha!" laughed the man. "My next blow will send you sailing down the stream!"

Robin had been surprised by the speed and power of the blow that hit him. But he was ready for the next one. He ducked as the two staffs met with a great crack above his head.

Both men advanced to fight at close quarters. To and fro they went; attacking and defending. Each blow that struck home had the other man teetering on the edge of falling into the river. Soon both were bleeding from several wounds. Yet, despite the stranger being far taller and broader than Robin, the fight was fairly equal. The contest went on.

After two hours of fierce battle on the tree trunk, they agreed to a short rest to have a drink of water. Then they set to again. The day wore on and still there was no victor.

"Are you ready to give up, stranger?" gasped Robin, as evening approached.

"Never!" replied the man, along with another whistling swing of his staff.

Robin was sure the man was tiring. He advanced for a final assault, bringing down his staff with the very last of his own strength. The blow should have broken the man's head, but he was ready for it. He swerved to the side and ducked down.

Robin's blow missed the mark completely and he was thrown off balance. He had almost recovered his foothold when the man delivered a slicing blow that knocked his legs from beneath him. With a desperate cry, he tumbled head-first into the river.

"How now!" laughed the stranger, when Robin bobbed to the surface. "Now will you let me pass first?"

Even Robin, still spluttering for breath, saw the funny side of it. He knew he had been beaten by a cleverer man. He was ready to admit it too. "If you don't give me a hand, I

The two staffs met with a great crack.

shall float all the way to Nottingham," he laughed.

The stranger hurried back along the bank and put out a hand for Robin to catch. "Generally, I wouldn't do this for any man," he said, "but you fought like a lion."

"I doubt there is any other man on earth who could have tipped me into the water as you did," replied Robin, gratefully accepting the hand.

As soon as Robin had dried himself, he asked the man's name.

"Men call me Little John," he replied, puffing out his huge chest and stretching himself to his full height of close to six feet and six inches.

Robin laughed again. "A fine name for one so small!"

That evening they returned to the Great Oak and took care of their battle wounds. Then they roasted some forest rabbits that Robin had caught the day before, and had a fine feast.

***

Little John was the first of what became known as Robin's "Merry Men". Next to join

Tumbling head-first into the river.

the band were Will Stutely and David of Doncaster – two good fellows who had fallen on hard times and been outlawed.

In the months that followed, others joined them. Most were outlaws for one reason or another. Many of them had a sheriff's price on their heads.

Some were wanted for killing the King's deer, but most were just poor people who had been forced to steal. It was the only way they could feed their starving families who had been robbed by the Sheriff of Nottingham's cruel henchmen.

Others had been robbed of their lands by the Sheriff's men. Some had been forced to sell their land to pay the Sheriff's high taxes.

In that first year in Sherwood, Robin gathered together some thirty outlaws. And by Robin's twentieth birthday, there were fifty men living in and around the Great Oak.

They were united by a hatred of injustice.

Robin was still young but the others – some older than him – chose him as their leader because none but Little John could match Robin's fighting and archery skills, or his bravery. Robin chose Little John as his right-hand man.

Robin made everyone swear never to harm a child or maid, wife or widow. They also had to vow to fight injustice and cruelty wherever they saw it.

And they promised no favors to the rich and the powerful, be they sheriffs, barons, knights, monks or church friars. If any of those wealthy men had stolen from the poor, they would be treated as common robbers.

Robin himself promised that any riches they took from these powerful robbers would be shared out among the poor and hungry.

Another thing all were agreed upon was that any traveler passing through Sherwood should be stopped and questioned. If they were wealthy and couldn't explain where their money had come from, then Robin and his men would take possession of it.

Robin set up a series of "watch trees" on all the main tracks through Sherwood Forest. Each member of the band took it in turn to spend a day hidden in one of these trees, watching the comings and goings in the forest. Nothing and nobody moved in Sherwood without Robin knowing about it.

One day Robin was taking his turn in one of the Watch Trees when a man dressed in an expensive-looking red cloak, and carrying an ancient quarterstaff in his hand, wandered down the track on foot.

Robin, his trusty quarterstaff at the ready, dropped from the branch where he had been hiding among the thick greenery.

"Stop where you are!" he shouted.

Chapter 5
Will Scarlet

The stranger didn't seem in the least concerned to see Robin appear so suddenly from the tree. "Why should I stop?" he said, continuing to walk towards him.

"Because you look rather too wealthy in that red cloak," said Robin. "Unless you can prove you came by your wealth honestly, you'll have to pay to pass by."

The man ignored Robin's warning. "I have no money," he said and continued to walk on.

Robin insisted that the man stop.

"Then I'll have to kill you," said the stranger, gripping his staff tightly.

"Put your staff away," said Robin, looking at the man's slender frame. "I could cut you in two like a barley straw."

"Then come and do it," said the stranger. "You'll find me the toughest straw you ever tried to cut!"

That was enough to raise Robin's temper. He

lashed out at the man with his staff. The stranger simply pushed the staff away and struck the outlaw a cracking blow with his own staff.

Now the two men faced each other like two angry bulls, and advanced to attack. And what a fight it was!

Soon after it began, Little John, Will Stutely and David of Doncaster arrived. None had ever seen such a battle.

"I think Robin will have a headache after this fight," said Little John. "He's met his match."

They continued fighting for an hour or more before the stranger caught Robin a fearful blow on the head. He fell to the ground, almost unconscious.

Little John ran forward. "Stop the fight, stranger. Robin is done for."

"A plague on you, Little John," cried Robin, recovering his wits again. "I'm not finished yet."

"Come Robin, admit it," said Little John. "You've been beaten by me with my staff and now you've been beaten by this man. Admit defeat!"

"Never!" cried Robin, finally getting to his feet and rubbing his sore head.

The two men came together again in an

"I could cut you in two like a barley straw."

explosion of blows. But once more the stranger got the better of Robin and knocked him to the ground. Little John and Will were laughing now.

"Robin, you may be the best archer in the land," said Little John, "but the staff is not your favorite weapon. Admit it!"

"Alright my friends," said Robin, smiling at the same time as rubbing his head, "I yield to the stranger! So tell me who is it that has given me such a sore head?"

"They call me Will Scarlet," said the man. "And who are you?"

As soon as Robin revealed who he was, Will Scarlet shook his opponent's hand. By now, there were few people in the forest who hadn't heard of Robin and his good deeds.

"A man with such skill with a staff," said Robin, "should come and join us. What say you, Will Scarlet?"

"The Sheriff's men killed my family and threw me out of my house," he replied, "so I shall be pleased to join you, Robin."

"Welcome, Will Scarlet," said Will Stutely.

"Come, Will," said Little John, "there's a feast of the King's deer waiting for us back at the Great Oak."

***

Will Scarlet

Will Scarlet shook his opponent's hand.

Over the next few months Robin's camp at the Great Oak grew and grew. Robin still slept in the Great Oak but he had now built a roof above his nesting place to keep out the rain.

Beneath the tree, several huts made of oak frames and covered with bark had been built for the others to sleep in. There was also a long rough-hewn oak table that Little John had built. Robin's entire band of men could sit around it.

Robin's men all dressed themselves in green tunics. The color was called Lincoln Green; a color that matched the green of the summer leaves exactly.

Close to the great table, a large fireplace had been dug into the ground. This was where the great joints of venison were roasted. At the very base of the tree was a special place where Robin stood when he talked to his men. It was also the place where any passing minstrel could sing

And how Robin's men liked to sing! They weren't known as Robin's Merry Men for nothing.

Chapter 6
The Archery Contest

As the months passed, Robin Hood became bolder and bolder. At times he would disguise himself and sneak into Nottingham Town. He even saw Marian on some of those dangerous visits. He desperately wanted to spend more time with her, but he dare not. If they were seen together they might both end up on the end of a gallows rope.

One day, the Sheriff of Nottingham heard about the secret visits that Robin made into Nottingham. It gave him an idea. If he could tempt Robin into the town on a particular day, he might capture him.

The Sheriff's idea was simple. He would announce an archery contest. Surely, Robin would never be able to resist a challenge like that.

Over the next few days, the Sheriff sent out soldiers to every village and hamlet to announce the contest. The prize would be a solid gold arrow!

By now Robin had won many friends across the countryside for the money he often brought to the poor. In turn, many of these people became Robin's spies.

So nothing that happened in the villages around Sherwood Forest escaped Robin's notice.

On the edge of Sherwood Forest stood an ancient tavern called the Blue Boar Inn. Robin and his men, often dressed in disguise, came here for a welcoming ale. The landlord, Tom Turnbull, and most of his customers, were not fooled by the disguises. But they would never think of turning Robin over to the Sheriff's men, who often drank there too.

If Tom or his customers overheard anything interesting, they would pass it on to Robin. In this way, Robin heard of the Sheriff's plan to trap him.

"'Tis a shame, you'll have to miss the archery challenge now," said Will Stutely. "They'll be waiting for you there."

"Never let it be said that I was scared of a Sheriff's plot," answered Robin. "The more I hear about it, the more I want to try for that archery prize. I shall meet trickery with trickery!"

***

Announcing the archery contest

On the day of the archery contest, Nottingham Town was crowded with people who had come to see the finest archers from miles around. Among them were Dick of Lincoln and Sir Guy of Gisborne – the Sheriff of Nottingham's best archer.

Sir Guy was a cruel, bully of a man. He did much of the Sheriff's dirty work. If the Sheriff told him to kill an enemy, the deed was done without another word. He had sworn to the Sheriff that one day he would capture Robin Hood.

The archery challenge was being held in the meadow outside the main town gate. The rows of benches soon filled up with knights and their ladies, squires and other high-ranking folk. The Sheriff of Nottingham arrived and took his place on a special throne erected at the front.

The poor folk arrived in their hundreds too. Never had such a large crowd come to see an archery contest!

The target was a small circular piece of wood fixed to a pole. It was marked with three black rings. The target was only twelve inches across and stood some one hundred and thirty yards from where the challengers were now waiting to begin.

The Sheriff examined the competitors one by one. He wanted to see whether Robin had turned up. He had never actually seen Robin before, but the foresters had given him a good description.

The Sheriff looked along the line of competitors. All but one were dressed in Lincoln green cloaks and hats. The Sheriff couldn't tell one from the other.

The one man who stood out was wearing a ragged scarlet cloak with a hood that covered

A large crowd came to see the contest.

his head. The Sheriff hardly bothered to look at him; he could have been a tramp.

"I can't see Robin," the Sheriff muttered to himself. "But I shall surely know him when he shoots his bow."

The first part of the contest was to reduce the huge number of challengers to just ten men. That was quickly done because only ten archers managed to hit the tiny target. The Sheriff eyed each one and sadly decided that Robin was not there.

The second part of the contest reduced the ten archers to just three – Sir Guy of Gisborne, Dick of Lincoln and the man in scarlet.

Dick was first man up. His arrow thudded close to the center of the target. Now it was Sir Guy of Gisborne's turn. He took careful aim, waited a moment and then released the bowstring. The arrow flew straight to the heart of the target.

"Who's closest so far?" called out the Sheriff.

A servant rushed out and measured the distance between the two arrows.

"Sir Guy is closest," he called back. "He's hit the center mark. He can't be beaten."

The stranger in the red cloak approached

The arrow thudded into the target.

the shooting mark. He pulled an arrow from his quiver, took aim and shot. What happened next astounded everyone there.

The arrow flew high into the sky, looped down and split Sir Guy's arrow into four pieces. The arrow thudded home into the target, dead center.

The crowd suddenly fell silent. They had never seen an archer split another man's arrow.

"Curses on the fellow!" muttered Sir Guy under his breath. He was a man who never liked to be beaten at anything.

Even the Sheriff had to accept that the man in scarlet had fairly won the contest. "What is your name?" he asked when the man came to collect his prize.

"They call me Jock of the North, sire," answered Robin.

"Then Jock, you are the finest archer I have ever seen," said the Sheriff. "Far better than that scoundrel, Robin Hood."

"Oh, there never was a more roguish scoundrel than Robin Hood," smiled Robin. "He deserves a good hanging!"

"Jock of the North," answered the Sheriff, "you're a man after my own heart. And one day you will see the man hang. I promise you that."

Robin smiled again.

"But first you must catch him, sire," he muttered, as he turned away.

Chapter 7
Robin Fools the Sheriff

That night in the Great Hall of Nottingham Castle, the Sheriff presented Jock of the North with his prize, the golden arrow.

"Jock," said the Sheriff, "you must come and join me. With your archery skills, we'd soon have that devil Robin Hood on the end of a rope."

"Oh, indeed, sire," replied Robin. "I could easily bring Robin to you. But, I can be no one's slave or servant. I promised my father before he died that I would always be my own master!"

The Sheriff always got his own way. No one would normally dare refuse any request he made. Yet, the boldness of the man in the scarlet cloak caught him off guard.

"I could hang a man for refusing me," he snorted. "But you are young and bold. I'll forgive you this once. Now be gone!"

Robin left the Great Hall and hurried away.

The Sheriff then called for his evening banquet to begin. While greedily taking great chunks of meat from a huge chicken leg, he started talking about Jock of the North. "He would have beaten Robin Hood even if the coward outlaw had dared to turn up," he chuckled.

At that very moment, an arrow flew through an open window and thudded into the floor right at the Sheriff's feet. The Sheriff was shocked. Who would dare to do such a thing? He pulled the arrow out. There was a note rolled around it. Slowly, he opened it and read the message.

"I give thanks for the golden arrow you gave me today. I am sorry I could not stay to celebrate with you. I have duties back in Sherwood Forest.
Robin Hood."

The Sheriff rushed to the window and looked out. It was too late. Robin Hood, still wearing the tattered red cloak, was galloping on a horse up the hill towards Sherwood Forest. He stood up in the stirrups, turned, and gave the Sheriff a final wave. Then he vanished into the trees.

"Curses on the man!" cried the Sheriff. "I shall have him hanging from the ramparts of this castle one day."

The Sheriff of Nottingham was furious at being fooled by Robin Hood. He sent out more patrols of soldiers into Sherwood Forest to track down the outlaw, but Robin's men, hiding in the watch trees, tracked their every move.

The Sheriff's soldiers often remarked how many owls there were in the forest that year. In fact, it was Robin's men signaling to each other, warning that another patrol was passing through.

Robin had only killed once in his life, and that was by accident. He had sworn that he would never kill again. He knew that the Sheriff's men were just ordinary folk who had been forced to work for the Sheriff. So he had nothing personal against them and wished them no real harm.

Still, that didn't stop him having his fun with them. Sometimes he and his men would surprise a patrol by dropping out of the trees and quickly disarming the soldiers. Then they would be tied up, sat back to front on their horses and sent back to the Sheriff.

The Sheriff was red-faced with anger when

Who would dare do such a thing?

this happened. He increased the reward for Robin's capture to five hundred pounds.

But not everything went Robin's way.

One day Will Stutely, as sly as any fox in Sherwood Forest, went to the Blue Boar Inn to see if there was any news to gather. He disguised himself by wearing a long monk's cloak over his normal Lincoln green. The garment hid his whole body and also, his trusty sword that hung from his belt beneath.

Will wasn't surprised to find several of the Sheriff's men drinking at the Inn. But he was shocked when he saw that the Sheriff of Nottingham was with them.

He sat down nearby, his staff in his hand and his head bowed forward as if he was meditating.

Even the landlord Tom Turnbull, who knew Will well, did not recognize him in the monk's clothes. But Tom's cat couldn't be fooled. Will always played with the cat when he came in. Now the cat started clawing at his cloak and accidentally lifted the hem, just enough to reveal his Lincoln green beneath.

The eagled-eyed Sheriff spotted the green immediately. He got up and approached Will. "Holy friar," he said, "pray tell me, where you are going on this fine summer day?"

Disarming the soldiers

"I am a pilgrim going to Canterbury Town to pray," answered Will, hoping his story would fool the Sheriff.

"Indeed," said the Sheriff with an evil smile crossing his lips. "And when did a friar wear Lincoln green?"

"Lincoln green?" said Will. "I am a friar. You'd be better off searching for Robin Hood's men if you're looking for Lincoln green."

"I think I am nearer to one of Robin Hood's villains than I have ever been," answered the Sheriff.

Will Stutely knew the game was up.

Chapter 8
Will Stutely Captured

Will Stutely leapt to his feet, only to find the Sheriff with his sword drawn, blocking his escape.

"Come now, I doubt you're a friar at all," said the Sheriff triumphantly. "You are one of Robin Hood's knaves. One move and I'll run you through. Take him, men!"

The Sheriff's soldiers quickly disarmed Will and tied him up.

"It's the gallows for you," sneered the Sheriff. "Or perhaps I might save your life if you can lead us to Robin's camp."

"Never!" cried loyal Will. "Hang me ten times and I still wouldn't betray my master."

That night Will was thrown into one of the Sheriff's dungeons in Nottingham Castle.

The news that Will had been captured reached Robin the next day. Robin ordered Little John to ride off to the Blue Boar Inn to see if there was any news of Will's fate. Little

John was back before sunset. The news was grim. Will was to be hanged the very next evening, on the gallows that stood outside the town walls.

"Loyal Will has risked his life for us," Robin said to his men. "Now we must risk ours to save him. We'll bring Will back or die with him!"

"Aye!" cried every man there.

Robin and his men spent the night talking about what they should do. By the time the sun rose the next day, a plan was set.

The next afternoon Robin and his men set off on foot for Nottingham. They traveled in twos or threes so as not to cause suspicion. By late afternoon they were all inside the town, ready to put their plan into operation.

The town had never been so busy. Will Stutely had been born in Nottingham and he was a much-liked man. Everyone was sad when he had been outlawed for stealing one of the King's deer. He had a family and three children to feed. So that evening all the good folk of Nottingham came out into the streets, to say a sad farewell to Will.

As the sun sank low over Sherwood Forest, bugles sounded from the walls of Nottingham castle. The castle gates opened and Will

"Take him, men!"

appeared, standing in the back of a horse-drawn cart. His hands were bound behind his back and a masked hangman was at his side.

Two columns of soldiers rode on either side of the cart. The Sheriff of Nottingham was riding beside it too.

"Well," grinned the Sheriff as he looked at poor Will. "Robin can't help you now."

"You shall pay dearly for this day's work," said Will proudly. "Good Robin will avenge my death. Little do you know how much he laughs when he talks of you and your cowardly ways."

The words hit their target. The last thing that the Sheriff wanted was to be seen as a figure of fun.

"I'm a jest with your master, am I?" he shouted. "Let's see how he laughs when I play a little gallows humor on you. It will be my turn to laugh when you swing!"

All the time, the crowd following Will was getting larger. People were already pressing in on the riders who were guarding him. As soon as they reached the main city gate, the Sheriff quickly rode off to take up his position close to the gallows.

Will saw the gallows and then lifted his eyes to look at the countryside beyond. He saw the

"Robin can't help you now."

sheep and their lambs in the fields where he had played as a boy. He could also see the house where he was born. Tears came to his eyes as he remembered the happy days of his youth. For a moment, he bowed his head so the crowd wouldn't see the tears.

Suddenly, the Sheriff shouted. "Get back! Get back!"

Will saw a giant of a man forcing his way through the crowds on one side of the cart. Then he turned to see another man doing the same on the other side.

His heart leapt with joy. The first man was Little John. The other was Robin Hood. And behind each man, all in a line, were the rest of the outlaws.

Chapter 9
Rescue!

The Sheriff of Nottingham watched helplessly as the two lines of Robin's men forced themselves between the cart carrying Will and the guards on horseback.

"Stand back you villains!" cried the Sheriff.

"Stand back yourself!" came the reply from the giant, who now found himself right beside Will's cart.

Little John leapt aboard. He toppled the hangman out of the cart with a flick of his arm and then cut the bonds holding Will.

"Take him! Cut them down!" screamed the Sheriff, suddenly realizing what was happening.

The crowd was now so thick that all of the Sheriff's guards were being forced away from the cart. The Sheriff dug his heels into the side of his huge black horse and galloped back towards it. With his sword flying in all directions, he cut a path through to the cart.

Little John leapt aboard

"A giant you may be," he shouted at Little John, "but the further you will fall."

The Sheriff rose in his stirrups and sliced at Little John.

Robin's man was ready. He ducked and the sword swished over his head. Then he kicked out with his boot and lifted the Sheriff out of his saddle and into the air. The Sheriff finally hit the ground, his sword bouncing into the air and dropping neatly into Little John's hand.

"I thank you sire," said the giant outlaw. "'Tis a handsome sword indeed. I shall be grateful if I can borrow it for a while."

"Kill them!" screamed the Sheriff, in a fury.

But such was the crowd that his soldiers had no idea where Robin and his men were any more. They were too busy trying to fight their own way out of the crowd. Even the man on the horse and cart had run for his life.

Will took charge of the cart. He grabbed the reins and cracked the whip. The horse galloped away, pulling the cart at speed through the crowd. How the crowd shouted and cheered as they saw Will and Little John racing away towards Sherwood Forest.

Robin and a few of his men had one last job to do. They caught hold of the gallows rope and

"'Tis a handsome sword indeed."

pulled the execution stage to the ground with a great crash.

"Farewell, Sheriff," cried Robin.

"This will cost you your life," roared the Sheriff. "Just you wait and see! And I'll bring Prince John to witness your death."

That night there was much celebrating around the Great Oak in Sherwood Forest. Robin's band of Merry Men feasted and sang songs well into the night.

***

There were quiet days in the forest after Will Stutely's rescue from the gallows. Robin became a little bored, with nothing to do but sit around the Great Oak eating, drinking, and thinking about Maid Marian.

"Right!" he cried one morning. "I can't sit here any longer. I'm going to find some adventure."

And before his men could say a word, Robin was off.

Not long after, he met a butcher who was on his way to Nottingham Market to sell his beef and mutton. His old horse-drawn cart was weighed down with all sorts of meats.

The butcher and his cart gave Robin an idea. "Good day to you, sir," said the outlaw.

The butcher looked frightened. He was already wondering if the man was Robin Hood.

"If you are Robin Hood, please don't rob me," he pleaded. "I am but an honest man trying to earn a living."

"I am Robin Hood," replied the outlaw, "but

Robin met a butcher.

you have nothing to fear from me. You may be able to help me."

"I have heard of your good deeds to help the poor," said the butcher. "I will help if I can."

Robin asked him how much he would expect to earn from selling his meat at the market that day. The butcher said perhaps ten pounds if it was a good day.

"If I give you twenty pounds, would you let me borrow your butcher's hat and apron, and your cart, and let me take your meat to market today?" asked Robin.

"It's a bargain," said the butcher, "but why do you want to go to town?"

"I'm in search of adventure," answered Robin. "And I might find it in Nottingham."

It was then that the butcher revealed to Robin that the Sheriff was holding a special feast for all of Nottingham's butchers that night, in the castle.

"I have no wish to dine with that monster," he said, "but perhaps you would."

It was the best piece of news Robin had heard all day. "I shall certainly go," he said. "Perhaps I can cause some merry mischief while I'm there . . ."

Chapter 10
Robin Dines with the Sheriff

Robin put on the butcher's hat and apron, and jumped aboard the cart. "I shall bring your horse and cart back tomorrow," he said to the butcher, setting off on the road to Nottingham.

When Robin reached the town he set up his stall with the other butchers, but instead of selling the meat, he started giving it away to the poor. Soon large crowds gathered around his stall. No one recognized him beneath his butcher's hat. They wanted to know why he was giving his meat away.

"I have more money than I need," said Robin.

At the end of the day he joined the other butchers as they went into Nottingham Castle for the annual feast. The greediest man in Nottingham – the Sheriff – had already heard about the butcher who was so rich that he was giving his meat away. He couldn't wait to find out more about the man and his wealth.

Robin Dines with the Sheriff

Giving away the meat

The Sheriff had still never seen Robin Hood close up before. Even when he had presented Robin with the golden arrow, the outlaw had kept his face well hidden beneath his scarlet hood. So the Sheriff had no idea he was staring his enemy in the face.

"What is your name, stranger?" he asked, first of all.

"Robert the Hob, sire," replied Robin.

"Well," said the Sheriff, "you seem a jolly fellow, Robert. And wealthy and generous, no doubt!"

"Not as generous as you, master," replied Robin. "Why, I heard you gave Robin Hood a golden arrow."

The Sheriff frowned. He didn't like being reminded of the day Robin Hood fooled him at the shooting match. But Robin wasn't finished.

"You know, Sheriff," he said, "if you want to catch Robin Hood you'll have to lose some of that fat around your waist and stop drinking so much fine wine. That will clear the dust out of your brain."

The Sheriff might well have sent the joking butcher to one of his dungeons for such a remark. But that evening he was more interested in finding out how wealthy the man was.

"What is your name, stranger?"

"Robert the Hob," he said, "you seem to be a man of great wealth."

Robin guessed that the Sheriff was only interested in getting his hands on that wealth. So he played along.

"Yes, I have a great fortune," he replied. "Why, among my treasures is the finest herd of cows for miles round. It's worth six hundred pounds or more. Perhaps you might be interested in buying it from me – at a special price, of course."

"What price would that be?" asked the Sheriff.

"I don't need the money really," replied Robin, "but shall we say half price; three hundred pounds?"

The greedy Sheriff wasn't going to lose such a great bargain. "Meet me at the city gates tomorrow and take me to see them," he said. "I'll bring the money."

So it was agreed. Little did the Sheriff know that Robin was setting a trap for him!

Robin returned to his men that night and told them his plan.

The Sheriff also had a plan. He had not forgotten Robert the Hob's joke about him being overweight from too much food and drink.

"That jest will cost the foolish butcher dear," he said to himself, after Robin had left. "I doubt the cows will cost me a penny when I'm finished!"

Chapter 11
A Very Expensive Meal

The Sheriff, guarded by six soldiers, met Robin the next day, as promised.

"The herd is not far off," said Robin, still wearing his butcher's hat and apron. "Follow me."

When they reached the edge of Sherwood Forest, the Sheriff looked a little nervous. "The sooner we are out of this accursed forest the better," he said. "Pray, preserve us this day from Robin Hood!"

"Have no fear," replied the outlaw, "I know of Robin Hood and I can promise that you are in no more danger from him this day than you are from me."

The Sheriff didn't see the wide smile on Robin's lips as he said the words.

Robin took them deeper into the forest. The Sheriff became more and more nervous with each step. At last they came on one of the great herds of deer in the forest.

A Very Expensive Meal

"The herd is not far off."

"There!" said Robin. "How do you like my herd of cows?"

"They are not cows!" exclaimed the Sheriff. "They are the King's deer."

"Oh dear," said Robin, with a great smile on his face. "So they are. I must have made a mistake."

Robin clapped his bugle horn to his lips and blew three blasts, loud and clear.

Suddenly, the forest became alive. Everywhere the Sheriff looked, there seemed to be members of Robin's band dropping out of the trees. He and his soldiers were quickly surrounded and disarmed.

"What's this villainy, knave?" the Sheriff cried.

"It's not villainy," said Robin, pulling off his butcher's hat and apron.

The Sheriff guessed the truth at last. He had at last come face-to-face with his greatest enemy. "You green-clad knave!" he exclaimed. "Your devilish bones will rot on the end of a rope one day!"

Robin just smiled. "Why are you so rude to me?" he asked. "I only brought you into the forest to join us in a feast. You like your food and drink so much. You'll enjoy the company.

Now tell your men to return to the castle."

The Sheriff hesitated for a moment. The last thing he wanted was to lose his men and be left alone in the forest.

"Either you send the men back," said Robin, "or I will throw you into the river to see if you float or sink."

The Sheriff was pretty certain he was too heavy to float. So he was easily persuaded that it

The King's deer

73

was better to order his men to ride back to the castle. Robin then blindfolded the Sheriff for the next part of the journey. The outlaw wasn't going to show his enemy the way to his camp.

The Sheriff fell silent as Robin led the party ever deeper in the forest. He was sure he was about to die.

At last they reached the Great Oak, where a feast had already been laid on the table. Robin removed the Sheriff's blindfold, sat him at his right-hand and called for the feast to begin.

The Sheriff ate very little that evening. He had lost his famous appetite. Yet it was the finest roast deer he had ever tasted, even if he imagined it might be the last meal he ever had. The sight of the golden arrow pinned to the Great Oak gave him indigestion, too.

Robin entertained the Sheriff right royally all evening.

It was almost dark by the time Robin announced it was time for the Sheriff to return home. "I guarantee you safe passage," he said.

The Sheriff, seeing that Robin wasn't going to kill him, was now thinking of traveling through Sherwood Forest in the dark. He didn't see how Robin could guarantee his life against being attacked by the ghosts and hobgoblins

A Very Expensive Meal

The Sheriff ate very little.

that he was sure haunted the darkest corners of the forest.

"Surely, it would be better for me to travel in the morning," he begged, looking nervous.

"Oh no!" replied Robin, with a smile. "A little night adventure in Sherwood Forest will be good for you."

Four of Robin's men bundled the Sheriff onto his horse.

"Oh and before you leave us," said Robin mischievously, "I think you have forgotten something."

"And what's that, you rogue?" asked the Sheriff.

"You forgot to pay for tonight's feast," said Robin.

"I never said I would pay," protested the Sheriff.

"It's only fair," said Robin. "You've robbed most of my men or their families at one time or other, in taxes or goods. It's time to repay them a little."

"I can't. I won't!" blustered the Sheriff. "I have no money!"

"Methinks you have," said Robin.

"And how much will it cost me?" said the Sheriff, knowing full well what the price would be.

"I think three hundred pounds would be a fair sum," laughed Robin. "The same amount you were going to pay for the cows."

The Sheriff didn't argue. He'd had enough. All he wanted was to get out of the dark forest and back to the safety of his castle. He took out a money bag from his pocket and threw it at Robin.

"And worth every penny," laughed Robin.

The Sheriff was red-faced with anger.

Robin blindfolded the furious Sheriff again and Little John and Will Scarlet escorted him out of the camp. They didn't take him far. Robin's orders were that the Sheriff was to be left in some lonely part of the forest and forced to find his own way home.

And that's what happened.

It was two days before the Sheriff finally found his way out of the forest. He was consumed with anger. He was even angrier when, soon after, he heard a wandering minstrel singing a new ballad beneath the walls of Nottingham Castle.

It was called: *The Day the Sheriff Dined with Robin Hood.*

The Sheriff ordered that any man heard singing the song should be flogged!

Chapter 12
Midge the Miller

Robin Hood's sense of humor often got him into trouble, especially when he was bored and wanted a bit of fun.

One day he was walking in Sherwood Forest with some of his men when he spotted a young miller driving a cart down the track towards them.

"What say you we have some fun with this man," said Robin. "Let's pretend we're common thieves and want to rob him."

Both Little John and Will Scarlet were ready for some mischief too. So as soon as the young man reached them, Robin cried out for him to stop.

"And who bids me stop?" asked the miller in a deep voice, growling like a dog.

"Never you mind!" answered Robin. "Now, perhaps you will be so kind as to hand over the sacks of flour you are carrying."

"I shall not!" cried the miller. "And I shall

"Hand over the sacks of flour."

tell you something else. This is Robin Hood's territory and if he finds you here robbing an honest miller, he'll give you a good old ding on the ear!"

Robin burst out laughing. "I fear Robin Hood no more than I do myself," he replied. "Now, first open your sacks of flour. It's likely that's where you hide your money."

Robin didn't see the tiny smile creep across the young man's face as he got off his cart and went to open one of the sacks.

"You're too clever for me," said the miller at last. "There is money in the sack. I will find it for you."

With that, he plunged his hands into the sack. The next moment he drew out two great handfuls of flour and threw it at Robin, Little John and Will Scarlet.

A white, dusty cloud descended on the three men. It filled their eyes and noses. Their throats became choked. The more they rubbed their eyes, the worse it became. Tears poured down their faces. They couldn't speak for spluttering or see for flour gluing their eyes shut.

Now the miller drew out his wooden quarterstaff and began laying into the three robbers. With every blow, a cloud of white flour

Thwack! Thwack! Thwack!

flew into the air. Thwack! Thwack! Thwack! Robin and his men could not see to defend themselves. They tried to get away but the miller followed them, still whacking them with his staff.

At last Robin called out for mercy. "Stop! Stop! It was just a joke. I am Robin Hood!"

"You're a lying knave," cried the miller, lashing the three of them again. "Brave Robin Hood never robbed an honest man!"

With that, he gave Little John another blow on the skull and Will Scarlet a cracked rib. Each time the three outlaws tried to clean their faces of the flour, the miller only powdered them again. In desperation, Robin grabbed his horn and blew a mighty blow.

A few minutes later, six of Robin's men burst out of the trees. At first they didn't know what was happening. All they could see were three ghostly figures covered in flour and being attacked by a fourth man racing around in a cloud of dust.

At last, they realized it was Robin, Little John and Will Scarlet. And they needed rescuing from a madman with a quarterstaff.

Robin had finally cleaned his eyes and he saw his fellow outlaws arrive. He told them to stay where they were. "It is our own fault," he said. "We only meant to have a little fun with this miller, but the joke has been on us."

Robin raised his hand to the miller in surrender. "Forgive us," he said. "I truly am Robin Hood. What is your name?"

The miller finally realized that it was Robin. "I am Midge the miller." he said. "I work with my father in the old mill at the edge of the forest. Please forgive me for giving you such a beating!"

"It was our own fault, Midge," said Robin. "And you are the mightiest Midge I ever saw."

That night Robin, Little John and Will Scarlet limped back into camp. Yet for Robin, it had been a valuable day. He had learned not to make fun at other people's expense.

Besides, he now had another member of his band. Midge the miller left his dusty old mill and joined Robin's Merry Men!

Chapter 13
Tim the Tanner

If any of Robin's men ever got into trouble, it was usually Little John. One day he was taught a lesson he never forgot.

It all began one hot summer's day. Little John, was lying asleep beneath the Great Oak. Will Scarlet was dozing by the stream. Robin had been sleeping high up in his tree when he suddenly jumped up.

"Wake up, you lazy lads!" he cried. "Come, Little John, I have a job for you."

Robin wanted Little John to go to Loxley, to give Maid Marian some flowers. "And make sure none of the Sheriff's men see you!" he warned.

Little John slowly got to his feet, yawned and set off with the flowers. After a while, he came to the place where one road went to Loxley and another towards the Blue Boar Inn.

Oh, how he was tempted that morning. He knew he should go straight to Maid Marian's.

Tim the Tanner

"Wake up, you lazy lads!"

But a little devil in his head was suggesting how nice it would be to have a cooling drink of ale at the inn.

The devil won. Little John set off for the inn. When he got there, he found several old friends drinking some fine ale. He quickly joined them. After much drinking and laughing, he realized it was almost midnight. He decided he would have to stay the night.

The next day Little John set off again with the flowers, which were now rather wilted. By then, Robin had heard news of his night at the Blue Boar . . .

On the road to Loxley, Little John met Tim the Tanner, a man who prepared leather. They were strangers to each other but, being in a bad mood from too much drinking, Little John fell into an argument with Tim. Each man took out his quarterstaff and they began to fight.

Just then, Robin came on the scene. He hid behind a bush and watched the fight. He was astonished to see that Little John was losing. Little John had never lost a battle of quarterstaffs with any man.

"That will teach him," laughed Robin, from his hideaway. "The next time I ask him to deliver flowers, he'll think twice about spending the night at the Blue Boar!"

At last Little John tumbled to the ground. Tim the Tanner advanced, ready to strike him again.

"Stop! Stop!" begged Little John, every bone in his body aching. "I yield!"

"You've had enough, have you?" asked the Tanner.

"Aye, that I have," sighed Little John.

"And you admit that I am the better man?"

"Aye," replied Little John.

He hid behind a bush

"And you won't go picking arguments with innocent travelers again?"

"I promise," said Little John.

At that moment, Robin burst out of the bushes. He was roaring with laughter.

He slapped Tim on the back in congratulation. "Well fought!" he cried. "Little John's a lazy rogue. He should have been in Loxley delivering flowers. Instead he slid off to the Blue Boar Inn for the night. You have taught him a valuable lesson."

Poor Little John staggered to his feet, holding his aching head. "It's a lesson well learned," he said. "I promise you it won't happen again."

In the end, the day turned out well for Robin. Tim the Tanner came and joined the Merry Men.

Chapter 14
Allan a Dale

The following week, Robin and his Merry Men were enjoying a delicious supper of roast venison at the big table beneath the Great Oak. As they ate, they heard the sweetest music coming from the forest.

Soon after, a young minstrel playing his lute appeared from the trees. He seemed to have no fear of walking straight into Robin Hood's camp.

"Good evening, minstrel," said Robin. "You're a brave man to wander into Robin Hood's camp. What brings you here?"

"My name is Allan a Dale. I come with a love song for Robin," answered the minstrel.

"A love song eh, Allan," replied Robin. "And who has sent this love song?"

"Fair Maid Marian," said the minstrel. "She wrote the words and I put the music to it."

"Then, my fine fellow," said Robin, "I am Robin and you may sing it to me."

Allan sang the song. It was a sad love song about the birds of Sherwood Forest and especially the one that Marian loved best, the Robin.

The song went:

Sweetly sings the Nightingale,
And the cuckoo in the dale.
But the robin I love dear,
Singing all the year.
Robin! Robin!
Merry Robin!
How I love you dear.

You could have heard a pin drop in the forest. All the Merry Men were enchanted with Allan a Dale's voice and his playing on the lute.

"Well sung Allan a Dale," said Robin when the minstrel finished. "You have the sweetest voice."

It gave Robin an idea. "I tell you what, good minstrel," he said. "Why don't you come to stay with us in Sherwood? You can sing to us when we are in need of being cheered up."

Allan a Dale was happy to stay with Robin and his men. But he had a favor to ask.

Allan a Dale

A young minstrel appeared.

"My own true love, fair Ellen," said Allan, "is being forced to marry Sir Guy of Gisborne, one of the Sheriff's men. Is there anything you could do to help?"

"That cowardly traitor!" cried Robin. "I would be delighted to help you. When and where is the marriage to take place?"

"This Saturday," said Allan, "at Forest Edge Church."

"So we have two days to prepare a plan," said Robin, delighted that another adventure lay ahead. "Allan, I promise you that Ellen will be yours sooner than you ever imagined."

At dawn on the Saturday, Robin told Little John to stay behind and prepare a feast. Then he and the others set off for Forest Edge Church, which stood beside a river on the edge of Sherwood Forest. By the middle of the day they had reached the place. They saw the church in the distance, on the opposite side of the river.

Robin and his men were a little surprised to discover a friar asleep on the near bank. He was lying on his back, a half eaten beef pie and a flagon of ale beside him.

Robin distrusted many of the friars and monks around Nottingham Town and Sherwood Forest. Often they were allies of the

A friar was asleep on the near bank.

Sheriff and Prince John. They had become rich doing work for the treacherous pair.

Robin whispered to his men to lie down and hide in the tall grass, and just observe the friar for a while. Eventually, the friar awoke. Not realizing that he was being observed, he plunged his hand into the half eaten beef pie.

"What a fine day this is," the friar mumbled to himself. "What a fine day for a fine friar to attack a fine beef pie!"

"Hey, you lazy loafer," called out Robin, suddenly. "Are they all as lazy as you in this part of the world?"

The friar nearly choked on his pie. He rolled over and looked up with a bleary eye, to find Robin standing above him. "Who dares disturb me on a summer's day?" he asked, struggling to his feet. "And who's been spying on me and my beef pie?"

The friar's head was as round as a ball. His hair was black but he had a huge circular bald patch right on top of his head. His cheeks were as red as a robin's breast. His eyes were deeply mischievous. He was wearing a friar's cloak which reached to the ground.

The friar couldn't have been more surprised to see the strangers staring at him.

Chapter 15
Friar Tuck

The friar wiped his face with a greasy hand and took a swallow from his flagon of ale. "And what right have you to wake me so rudely?" he asked.

"I have a question for you," said Robin, pointing to the church on the other side of the river. "Are you the friar who belongs to yonder church?"

"I am – my name is Friar Tuck," he replied. "I haven't any time to spare for you. I have a marriage to conduct this evening. So be gone with you."

At that moment, Robin drew out his sword and started to play a favorite trick of his; tickling his enemy's nose with the point of his deadly weapon.

"If that's how you feel," said the friar, trying to get his nose away from the sword point, "I had better do as I'm told!"

"I see there is no bridge here," said Robin.

Tickling friar's nose

"Perhaps you will do me the courtesy of carrying me across."

"If you insist," said Friar Tuck.

Robin put his sword back in his belt.

Friar Tuck didn't like being used as a carthorse, but he walked to the riverbank and stooped down so Robin could clamber onto his back. Once aboard, the friar stepped into the water and carried Robin across.

But wily old Friar Tuck was no fool. As they crossed, he managed to loosen Robin's sword. When Robin jumped down on the other side, he found the friar tickling his nose with his own sword.

"Perhaps you will now do me the honor of carrying me back across the river," said Friar Tuck, with a huge smile on his face. "I want to finish my pie, if that is alright with you."

Robin had no choice. Now it was his turn to wade into the river with the friar on his back. Never had Robin carried such a load! All the way across, the friar dug his heels into Robin's ribs as if he was riding a horse.

Once across the river, the friar politely thanked Robin. "Now," he said, "please leave me to finish my pie and to have a sleep. As I said, I have a wedding to attend to later."

Just then Robin's men emerged from the long grass where they had been hiding. They were all laughing at how Robin had been forced to carry the friar across.

Now it was Robin's turn to smile as Will Scarlet stepped forward and took hold of Friar Tuck by the collar of his robe.

"We are due at the very same wedding you are going to," he said, lifting the very fat friar off his feet. "And none of us would like to get our clothes wet. Perhaps you would be so kind as to carry us all across."

The friar carried Robin across.

Friar Tuck wasn't going to argue with Will. For the next half hour, he carried Robin and his men – one by one – across the river.

Once they were all safely across, Robin took the friar aside. "Now my good Friar Tuck," he said. "I suspect the marriage you are about to perform is between Sir Guy of Gisborne and the fair maid Ellen."

"That is true, sir," answered friar. "But please don't delay me any more. If I'm not there to carry out the wedding, the Sheriff will hang me!"

"I wouldn't dream of keeping you from the wedding," said Robin. "But you can do me one more favor."

"I have done enough for you," said Friar Tuck. "Just leave me to do my wedding."

Once more Robin produced his sword. "You can either help me, or have this tickle your nose again!"

The friar knew he was beaten. "Who are you, sir?" he asked at last.

"Do you know the name Robin Hood?"

Friar Tuck suddenly smiled. "Robin Hood! By George! Why didn't you tell me that in the first place?" he said. "I would have been proud to carry you across the river."

Lifting the friar off his feet.

Suddenly they heard the sound of splashing, coming from further up the river. "It's the Sheriff!" cried Friar Tuck. "And Sir Guy and maid Ellen. I must get to the church and be ready to meet them."

Robin took the friar aside and whispered a few words to him in private. When he had finished, Friar Tuck put his finger to his lips, as if to say he could keep a secret. "I'll be ready!" he said.

***

That evening Friar Tuck stood by the altar in his church, ready to begin the wedding ceremony.

"Get on with it!" growled the Sheriff. "I have a feast in Nottingham Castle tonight."

"Yes, be quick," said Sir Guy of Gisborne.

The only person who wasn't happy for the service to begin was fair Ellen. There were tears pouring down her cheeks.

"Be quiet!" snapped Sir Guy. "If you're going to be my wife, you'll have to stop blubbering, girl."

The friar was about to begin, when the door at the back of the church slowly opened.

"Good evening," said Robin, his head appearing from behind the door. "Please excuse me for interrupting the wedding."

Chapter 16
A Wedding

"Who are these knaves?" asked Sir Guy, seeing Robin and his men coming into the church.

The Sheriff knew exactly who they were. He was speechless for a moment.

"No one will come to any harm," said Robin, "if you just do what you are told. Methinks the maid Ellen belongs to another. She is not yours to marry, Sir Guy."

The truth slowly dawned on Sir Guy. His thoughts turned to the day of the archery contest when he had been beaten by the man in the red cloak. "Why, it is young Robin Hood again," he sneered. "You made a fool of me once with your bow and arrow. Now you come to claim my bride."

At that moment the Sheriff called out to his soldiers, who were waiting at the other end of the church. "Kill them! Five hundred pounds to the one who brings me Robin Hood's head!"

The church echoed to the clanging of swords

A Wedding

"Who are these knaves?"

being drawn and the jangling of spurs as the Sheriff's men advanced down the aisle. Robin's men were ready. The battle began. And never was there such an unholy battle in a church!

The Sheriff's men charged at the outlaws, who escaped by dancing across the church benches. The chase was on. Mayhem broke out as Robin's men raced their way around the church, darting in now and then to crack a few Sheriff's men across the head.

One by one, the Sheriff's soldiers ran from the church in terror, leaving the Sheriff, Sir Guy, Ellen and Friar Tuck alone by the altar. Robin now advanced up the aisle, slowly and purposely, circling his sword in front of him. Sir Guy came forward, his sword at the ready.

Now the two men met, with a noisy clash of swords. Sir Guy was a good swordsman and the fight was an equal one, the pair advancing and retreating in turn.

Either man could have won the fight, but then Friar Tuck gave Robin a slight advantage. As Sir Guy retreated down the aisle, the friar untied a rope that held a large metal lamp high in the roof of the church. Slowly he lowered it to the ground.

Sir Guy didn't see the lamp until it was too

late. He backed into it and got caught up in the metal work. Now Friar Tuck pulled sharply on the rope, sending Sir Guy flying up to the roof with the lamp. He secured the rope and left Sir Guy hanging helplessly from the lamp.

The Sheriff knew it was time to leave. He ran for his life. Once more Friar Tuck joined the game. He stuck out a foot and sent the Sheriff tumbling to the ground.

Robin looked down at the Sheriff and placed the point of his sword on his large belly. "I'm pleased to see you're leaving, as you are not required here any longer," he said. "I have a wedding to attend now. And you are not on the guest list. Be gone!"

The Sheriff got to his feet and dashed out of the church.

Ellen was still in shock when Robin approached her. "Have no fear, Ellen," he said quietly. "We have come for your wedding."

Ellen was completely confused. "Who are you? Who am I to marry now?"

Robin turned and spoke to Will Scarlet. "Will, go and fetch the bridegroom!"

Will left the church and returned a moment later with Allan a Dale. Ellen burst into tears again and rushed into Allan's arms.

Hanging helplessly from the lamp

A Wedding

"Right, Friar Tuck," said Robin. "Now you can start the proper wedding."

And so Allan a Dale and Ellen were married by Friar Tuck in Forest Edge Church, by the river.

Afterwards they all traveled back to the Great Oak in Sherwood Forest, where Little John had prepared a great wedding feast.

The singing and dancing continued until dawn the next day.

And that was how Allan a Dale and Ellen came to live in Sherwood with Robin Hood.

Chapter 17
Little John at Nottingham Fair

When news of the wedding incident got about Nottingham Town, the Sheriff knew he had once again been made to look like a fool by Robin and his Merry Men. Ever since he had been robbed of three hundred pounds for his supper in Sherwood Forest, he had banned any mention of Robin Hood's name in his presence. Yet he knew the townsfolk whispered about Robin.

Now he was unsure what to do about the great Nottingham Fair that was normally held every year. An archery contest was always the main attraction. Archers from across the whole country would come to show off their skills.

The Sheriff well remembered how Robin had come in disguise and won the last great archery tournament.

At first, he thought he might cancel the event. But then he realized people might think he was scared of Robin Hood. What he decided to do was to hold the event, but offer an archery prize so valueless that Robin couldn't be bothered to come.

The prize he decided on was free firewood from Sherwood Forest for a single winter.

Robin laughed when he heard the news. "What's the point of my winning that, when I have free firewood all around me for the taking!"

But soon after, Little John, suitably disguised as an old ploughman, arrived back from a visit to the Blue Boar Inn. He had explained how he overheard some of the Sheriff's soldiers talking about how the prize was meant to keep Robin away.

"Robin," said Little John. "If they want to keep you away, let me go! I would love to have a match against Sir Guy and his friends."

"Let me go!"

Robin agreed. When the day arrived, Little John set off for Nottingham dressed in a scarlet cloak and hood, and with a new name for the day. He called himself Reynold Greenleaf. He carried a wooden quarterstaff in his right-hand and his bow and quiver of arrows over his shoulder.

The contest was being held on the green outside Nottingham's main gate, and was attended by hundreds of people out to enjoy the day. There was plenty of good ale to be drunk and Little John had his share. There was also a bout or two of wrestling between drinks. And Little John knocked a few heads together.

There was dancing too. Little John was a handsome man, broader and taller than most other men. So the lassies took their chance to dance with him.

After he had danced himself dizzy and broken the hearts of half a dozen lovesick ladies, he looked around for a man to fight with his staff. The man he came across was Eric of Lincoln.

"Hello, you long-legged country bumpkin," called Eric. "Have you the heart for a fight?"

"It would give me great pleasure," answered Little John, "to crack the head of a saucy braggart!"

A bout or two of wrestling

"Saucy braggart, eh?" snarled Eric, who was famed across the whole county for his fighting with a staff. "I'll rattle the teeth in your head if you'll come and fight."

No further invitation was needed. The two men leapt at each other as a huge crowd gathered around them to watch the coming battle. And how they cheered Eric! They fully expected him to lay out the man in the red cloak.

Eric was a powerful fighter, yet Little John had the bigger brain. He decided to play a game with his opponent. When Eric attacked, Little John took one step back. Then, as Eric carried on forward, Little John gave him a sharp crack on the head and retreated another step. He never gave Eric a chance to get close to him.

Little John's blows sent Eric into a fury. And the longer the battle went on, the angrier Eric became. Finally, he lost his temper completely. He charged like a wild man at his opponent, flailing at him with a storm of blows from his staff.

But he was too wild to hurt Little John, who calmly waited for his moment. Then he gave Eric a blow to the skull that sent him spinning across the grass. Eric lay unconscious as the crowd roared; this time in support of Little John.

He charged like a wild man at his opponent.

News of the defeat of Eric quickly reached the Sheriff, who came to see the victor. When he reached Little John, he stared at him closely.

"Surly, we have met before," said the Sheriff suspiciously, "I recognize your face."

Little John just laughed. "You probably have, my lord," he replied, looking steadily into the Sheriff's eyes, "but it's only because I live in Nottingham and have seen you so many times before, too."

"Maybe, maybe," said the Sheriff.

"Men call me Reynold Greenleaf," said Little John. "I'm told some men sing of my strength in ballads. I think your champion, Eric of Lincoln, will sing of my strength in years to come too."

The Sheriff smiled. "Eric is well-beaten," he said. "I shall need a new champion now. I think you could fill the role. What say you, brave Reynold Greenleaf?"

For a moment, Little John was struck dumb. Robin Hood's right-hand man was being asked to join the Sheriff! Then he quickly accepted the offer. He smiled all the way back to Nottingham Castle.

Chapter 18
Little John Goes to Work for the Sheriff

Little John's new job suited him perfectly, as he could be a spy for the outlaws. So he sent a message to Robin, to tell him what he was doing. In those first few days at the castle, one or two soldiers wondered whether they had met "Reynold Greenleaf" before. But no one suspected his real identity.

Little John found his new job rather easy. He sat close to the Sheriff's right-hand during feasts and rode out hunting with him. So apart from eating, drinking, hunting and sleeping as much as the Sheriff, there was very little to do.

Sometimes, when he got bored, Little John's humor got the better of him. Once, he pretended to the Sheriff that he'd heard in the Blue Boar Inn that Guy of Gisborne was a traitor, about to join Robin Hood's men. Of course, the Sheriff immediately arrested his strongest ally, clapped him in irons and threw him into a dungeon.

A few days later, Little John apologized to the Sheriff and admitted he had been given false information. When Guy of Gisborne was released, he swore to take his revenge on Reynold Greenleaf. But there was little he could do.

Mostly, Little John sent messages to Robin about the Sheriff's plans and movements . . . and ate. He ate so much that he grew to the size of an ox. And he took to sleeping in, staying in bed till late in the morning.

One morning the Sheriff had gone out hunting early, leaving Little John to sleep. When he awoke late in the afternoon, the sun was pouring through his window and the birds were twittering outside.

Little John just lay there, thinking how sweet and comfortable life had become. As the Sheriff's right-hand man, he could ask for anything at any time.

He leapt from his bed and thundered downstairs, his weight straining every wooden step.

In the kitchen, he met Robert the cook. "Give me my breakfast," he roared.

"So, Master Reynold Greenleaf," said

Little John found his new job rather easy.

Robert angrily, "now you ask for your breakfast in the afternoon! He that oversleeps cannot expect his breakfast. It is the early bird that catches the worm."

Little John was furious. "Go fetch my breakfast," he shouted, "or I'll break your bones."

"Your breakfast is in the larder," snapped the cook.

"Then fetch it for me!" said Little John.

"Fetch it yourself," answered Robert. "I'm not your slave."

"I say go and get it for me," repeated Little John.

"And I say fetch it for yourself!"

Little John marched across the room towards the larder. He tried to open the larder door. It was locked. The cook began to laugh. Little John looked around and saw him rattling the keys.

Little John's temper finally got the better of him. He took a step back and charged at the door. The door burst from its hinges and crashed to the floor.

Then he turned on Robert and knocked him senseless with a blow to the head with a frying pan.

"Take that as a warning," he cried. "Never

"Give me my breakfast!"

keep a hungry man from his breakfast."

But at that moment he suddenly felt a pang of guilt. In truth, he wasn't angry at the cook. He was really angry at himself for being so lazy and greedy. He was just taking out his guilt on the cook. Deep down, he yearned to be back in Sherwood Forest with Robin Hood and his Merry Men.

"Here I am grown fat and lazy," he said to himself. "Why, even the Sheriff could beat me at wrestling now."

Little John picked up the cook and placed him on a chair. When he recovered, he apologized for his temper. "You are right, Robert," he said. "I have grown fat and lazy. I dread to think what Robin Hood would think."

"Robin Hood?" said the cook, quite puzzled. "Robin Hood is a hero. I would rather I was cooking for him. Why should you worry what he thinks?"

Little John thought that Robin might be able to use a cook. He decided to trust the man. "My real name is Little John," he confessed.

"Why, I should have known it!" said the cook. "There can only be one man of your size in the county. I would give my life to be Robin Hood's cook in Sherwood Forest."

"Then you shall be," said Little John. "But we can't leave the castle until after tonight's grand banquet for Prince John."

Prince John was a regular visitor at Nottingham Castle and that night, Little John was to discover why.

Chapter 19
Astounding News

Trumpeters on the battlements of Nottingham Castle announced the arrival of Prince John, brother of King Richard the Lionheart and a man determined to steal his brother's throne.

That night, all the rich and powerful people of the county joined the banquet in the Prince's honor. Each one knelt at Prince John's feet and promised to serve him should he ever become King in his brother's place.

At the banquet, Little John, as usual, sat on the Sheriff's right-hand side. The Sheriff sat at Prince John's right hand. Even though the two men dropped their voices to whispers at times, Little John could hear everything the two greedy traitors said.

Soon after the banquet began, Prince John gave the Sheriff some astounding news of King Richard.

"Richard's been captured!" whispered the Prince, "on his way back from the Holy Land."

The arrival of Prince John

"Who by?" hissed the Sheriff.

"Duke Leopold of Austria, no less," said the Prince.

"But how long will he be a prisoner?" asked the Sheriff.

Prince John laughed. "As long as I keep paying the Duke to hold him in a dungeon. And as long as you keep taxing the poor so I can keep paying him to keep him there."

The Sheriff rubbed his hands. "I shall be introducing some new taxes this very week," he said. "And I hope that in due course, when you become King, there will be some reward for my efforts."

"My dear Sheriff," said Prince John. "Whichever way this all works out, you can be sure that you and I will end our days in the Tower of London. We will live there either as King of England and Lord High Sheriff, or waiting in a dungeon for my brother Richard to chop off our heads for treason!"

***

When the banquet was approaching its end, Little John hurried to speak with Robert in the kitchen.

"We must wait until everyone is asleep," he said, "and then we'll let ourselves out of the castle. We'll be with Robin by morning."

The two men sat in the kitchen waiting for Prince John and the Sheriff to go to bed. They were still drinking and laughing in the great hall.

"We're wasting our time here," smiled Little John. "Perhaps we should use the opportunity to take some of the Sheriff's silver before we go."

"A fine idea," laughed Robert. "Do you know where it's kept?"

"Certainly," said Little John. "As his trusted servant, I have a key to his treasure room!"

The two men hurried away to the depths of the castle, where the Sheriff's treasure room lay locked behind a great oak door. Little John produced the key and soon the door squeaked open.

The room was filled with sacks of silver and gold coins. It was all money that the Sheriff had stolen in taxes from the poor people. There was too much for the two of them to carry away, but they had an idea. One tiny barred window looked out across the castle moat.

"We can load up one cart with the sacks," said Little John excitedly. "We can take those with us. The rest we can drop out of the window into the moat. The Sheriff will never realize

The Sheriff's treasure room

that much of his treasure lies underwater, just inches from his nose. We can return when we want to take it away."

It took them almost an hour to drop the great bulk of the treasure into the moat. Then they gathered up twenty sacks of gold and silver to take with them.

It was dead of night by the time the Sheriff and Prince John finally went to bed and collapsed into a deep sleep. Little John and Robert loaded the sacks onto a cart and harnessed a horse to it. Then they were on their way.

"Who goes there?" cried the guard when they reached the main gate.

"Open the gate," shouted Little John. "We are on the Sheriff's business!"

The guard recognized the Sheriff's right-hand man and let down the drawbridge immediately.

The horse and cart clattered over the bridge. Little John expected the alarm to be raised at any moment. But at last they were clear of the bridge. He took one last look back at the castle. The guard had already raised the drawbridge again and the castle was as quiet as a grave . . .

Chapter 20
The Sheriff's Plan

It was almost daylight by the time Little John and Robert reached the Great Oak in Sherwood Forest. Little John took out his horn and blew a loud blast.

For a moment, Robin and his men thought they were under attack. Then Robin saw the broad shape of his old friend. He leapt down from the Great Oak and landed at Little John's feet.

"Welcome home!" cried Robin. "What news?"

First, Little John introduced Robert the Cook. Then he revealed what was hidden in the cart. The huge amount of silver and gold astounded Robin. He was even more surprised when Little John told him that more of the Sheriff's hoard was just waiting to be collected from the bottom of Nottingham Castle's moat.

Then Little John got to the truly important news. "King Richard has been captured by

Robin was astounded.

Duke Leopold of Austria," he announced, "and Prince John, with the Sheriff's help, is paying him to keep the King there forever. No doubt Prince John will soon proclaim himself as King of England."

"Traitorous villains!" cursed Robin. "They'll not succeed in this plan if I have anything to do with it."

Robin thought long and hard about what he could do to help King Richard.

At last he decided on a plan. He would send Will Stutely and thirty of his men on a long journey to France. From there they would head south to Austria and seek out Duke Leopold's castle.

"There are five bags of silver for you, Will," said Robin, "if you can find a way of rescuing the King!"

That very morning Will and his men set off on the long and dangerous mission. The life of the real King of England, Richard the Lionheart, depended on its success.

***

The Sheriff was furious when he discovered that Reynold Greenleaf and the cook had robbed his treasure house. He became even angrier when the true identity of Reynold Greenleaf was revealed to him as Little John.

In turn, Prince John was equally furious with the Sheriff. He cursed the Sheriff for being so foolish. "How could you allow an outlaw to become your most trusted servant? And how are you going to pay me to keep King Richard in Austria now? All the money's gone!"

A long and dangerous mission

Robin Hood

The Sheriff promised to raise new taxes immediately. "I shall squeeze the poor 'til their buttons burst," he cried. "I shall soon have my treasure house full again."

"And what about Robin Hood?" roared Prince John. "Are you going to let him rule Sherwood Forest forever?"

"I have a plan to catch Robin Hood," said the Sheriff. "I promise you that within the month he will be in this very castle."

"But can you keep him in your castle long enough to hang him?" bellowed Prince John.

"Have faith in me," said the Sheriff. "I have discovered that there is a person who the outlaw will risk all for."

"And who is that?" asked the Prince.

"Maid Marian!" the Sheriff replied. "She is Robin's childhood sweetheart. She will be my bait to capture him."

Prince John smiled. "You may be more cunning than I thought!"

Later that night, the Sheriff's soldiers went to the village of Loxley and arrested Marian.

Prince John and the Sheriff happily welcomed her to the castle.

"Don't worry," the Sheriff said to Marian, "we shall not be holding you in a dungeon. You

"You will be a guest of honor."

will be a guest of honor. Oh, I forgot to tell you. We'll be inviting Robin Hood to pay us all a visit!"

***

The news of Maid Marian's arrest quickly reached the Blue Boar Inn. One of Robin's supporters ran all the way to the Great Oak to break the bad news.

Just as the Sheriff had guessed, Robin's first thought was how to rescue Marian. That night, he and his men sat down to plan what to do.

It was late winter now and a huge fire was blazing in the camp. Around that fire sat Robin, Little John and Will Scarlet.

"The Sheriff will be waiting for you," warned Will Scarlet. "He is using Marian to lure you to your death."

"He will try," said Robin. "But I would rather risk all for Marian than do nothing. What say you, Little John?"

"I know Nottingham Castle better than anyone," answered Little John. "There is a way in that might not be guarded."

"Tell me more!" cried Robin.

The three men leaned closer as Little John broke into a whisper. "There is a tiny window," he began. "If we can reach it, we might be able to make a surprise attack."

The three men talked long into the night. At last their plan was ready. All they had to do now was to decide when to put it into operation.

Once more it was information gathered at the Blue Boar Inn that gave them an idea. The Sheriff was to hold a banquet for Prince John's birthday.

"What better day to surprise the Sheriff?" said Will Scarlet.

"It's as good a day as any," agreed Robin. "Come on my brothers, let's drink to our success."

Three drinking horns were produced and filled with foaming ale.

Robin raised his horn. "Good luck and long life to all of us!

"Aye!" echoed Little John, Will Scarlet and Allan a Dale.

Chapter 21
Robin in Nottingham Castle Again

Prince John's birthday banquet took place a few days later. Guests arrived from all corners of the kingdom.

Robin, Little John and Will Scarlet, disguised as monks, reached Nottingham early that morning. They rode into town on an old cart pulled by a donkey. It was a freezing day and snow was falling thickly.

Inside the castle, Prince John was talking with the Sheriff. "Will this be the day when Robin comes?" he asked.

"There are rumors that he is already in Nottingham," said the Sheriff. "If he does try and get into the castle, I am ready for him. He will be caught like a fly in a spider's web."

"A fine birthday present he will be too!" sneered the Prince. "Especially if I can hang him from the battlements."

Prince John's birthday banquet.

"The honor will be yours!" laughed the Sheriff.

The banquet began early in the evening, inside the Great Hall of Nottingham Castle. The room was filled with long wooden tables and benches which seated all of the five hundred guests.

Prince John sat on the most important table, closest to the roaring fire. The Sheriff was sitting on one side of him. Sir Guy of Gisborne sat on the other. Beside Sir Guy sat Maid Marian. The Sheriff had decided that she should be Sir Guy's bride.

There was no one more miserable in the hall that night than Marian.

"Bring on the food!" roared the Sheriff. "Let the musicians play!"

Immediately, long lines of servants appeared in the hall. They carried huge platters filled with every delicacy. There were great joints of roast beef and pork, delicious veal and game birds such as pheasant, partridge and duck.

High up in the roof of the Great Hall, a giant of a man looked down on the banquet and licked his lips.

"What I wouldn't give for a slice of that

roast beef!" laughed Little John.

"We have work to do before you can fill that stomach of yours," replied Robin, who was right behind Little John with Will Scarlet.

Under cover of the snowstorm, the three men had used a rope to climb up onto the battlements. From there, they had crept unseen to a tiny window above the Great Hall. Now they were inside and hiding in the rafters right above the top table, where Prince John and all the important guests were sitting.

Robin and Will Scarlet each tied one end of a rope around their waists. The other ends were tied to the main roof beam above them. The rest of the rope was coiled up beside them.

Meanwhile, Little John carefully placed one arrow in his bow and put two others beside him, ready to use.

Just then, a drop of melted snow ran down Robin's cloak and dropped into space. Down, down and down it went, finally splashing onto Prince John's forehead.

The Prince immediately looked up. For a split second all he could see was dark shadows in the eaves of the roof. Slowly the shadows took form. "Strangers in the roof!" he screamed.

"Strangers in the roof!"

The Sheriff and Sir Guy looked up.

The Sheriff knew instantly who was up in the roof. He was delighted. "Welcome to my banquet!" he called out. "Do come and join us. Best to have a good meal before a good hanging."

"I shall be delighted to join you," Robin shouted down. "Here I come!"

With that, he and Will took hold of the coils of rope and threw them into the air. They tumbled down until they reached the floor.

In an instant, Robin and Will were sliding down the ropes – at the same time as Little John shot his first arrow.

Chapter 22
Robin Takes the Sheriff by Surprise

Robin and Will slid down the ropes and crashed onto the Sheriff's table, sending plates and cups, and legs of beef and joints of mutton flying in all directions.

At the same time Little John's first arrow, shot from above, nailed the sleeve of the Prince's coat of gold cloth to the table.

A second arrow pinned Sir Guy of Gisborne's cloak to his chair. He tried to get up to take out his sword, but he was caught by the arrow. Maid Marian took her chance and put out her foot. Sir Guy tripped and tumbled to the floor with the chair on top of him.

A third arrow nailed the Sheriff's boot to the floor, narrowly missing his big toe. "Guards!" he screamed, getting up from his chair and leaving the boot still fixed to the ground.

Sir Guy tripped and tumbled to the floor.

143

Prince John was also calling for the guards and struggling to free himself from Little John's arrow. Robin and Will's sudden arrival from the roof had taken everyone by surprise.

Robin grabbed Maid Marian and spun his rope around her waist, and signaled to Little John. In a moment, the giant outlaw had whisked her into the air and up into the roof. For a man so strong, it was like lifting a feather.

With Marian safely in the roof, Little John dropped the rope back to Robin.

Robin had now drawn his broadsword, ready for the approaching guards. By the time the guards reached him, Will Scarlet, his rope now wrapped around his waist, had already taken up a defensive position in front of his master.

"Time to fly, Will!" cried Robin, signaling to Little John.

Will Scarlet's weight was no problem for Little John. Using one of the great roof beams as a pulley, he whisked his fellow outlaw into the air and up into the roof.

Robin was now fighting off the guards with his sword, waiting for his moment. At last Little John landed Will safely and grabbed Robin's rope. Up Robin flew, like an eagle, to the safety of the rafters.

144

Up Robin flew, like an eagle.

Now the Great Hall was in mayhem. The Sheriff and Prince John were screaming orders in all directions.

"To the battlements, men," shouted the Sheriff.

The soldiers raced away to climb up to the battlements with the Sheriff and Prince John behind them. They were sure they had Robin trapped now. But even as they climbed upwards, Robin and the others were already on their way down, using a secret passage that Little John knew about.

So, as the Sheriff's men raced upwards, Robin, carrying Marian in his arms, and with Will and Little John behind him, scampered down into the depths of the castle to a secret door. There were two guards on the door, but they were only too happy to let Robin pass.

The tiny door opened onto the castle moat. And there was Allan a Dale, waiting with a small rowing boat. In a few minutes, they had vanished into the snowstorm and reached the other side of the moat.

The Sheriff and Prince John reached the battlements to find no sign of Robin.

"Curse this snow!" cried the Sheriff. "We'll never find them in this."

"Curse you, that's what I say!" snarled Prince John. "You've let Robin escape again."

Back in Sherwood Forest, the celebrations went on long into the night as everyone huddled around the roaring fire beside the Great Oak. Robin was the happiest man in Sherwood Forest, now that Maid Marian was with him.

Chapter 23
The Surprise Wedding Guest

The last of the winter months passed quickly. Soon the spring sunshine warmed Sherwood Forest again. The bare winter trees began to show the first green of the season as new buds appeared on the branches.

Robin was not worried about being attacked by the Sheriff. His soldiers had spent the winter in the castle. Even if they had dared to venture into Sherwood, they would have discovered that Robin had more men in his band than ever. The further Robin's fame spread, the more people came to join him.

There was one thing, though, that Robin was concerned about. He had still heard no word of Will Stutely and the others who had journeyed to Europe in search of King Richard the Lionheart.

The days passed quietly, with Robin and Marian often walking together, alone in the depths of the forest.

"It seems so long ago," said Marian one day, "when we lost each other after you killed that deer."

"Indeed it does," replied Robin. "We must never lose each other again."

It was then that Robin knew he had to ask Marian a question. "Will you marry me?" he asked quietly.

Marian didn't hesitate with her answer. "Of course I will."

Robin took Marian in his arms and threw her into the air with joy. Marian laughed as she tumbled back down to him again.

That night the outlaws' camp in Sherwood Forest rang to the sound of happy dancing, laughter and feasting. Allan a Dale sang a new love song he had written for the pair. Then Friar Tuck suggested that he should marry them at Forest Edge Church.

"Who will carry us across the river?" joked Robin, remembering the day he and Friar Tuck had first met.

"I will willingly get my feet wet for you and Marian," laughed the Friar. "It will be my wedding present."

"Well said!" replied Robin.

"Will you marry me?"

Two weeks later, almost one hundred of Robin Hood's Merry Men gathered at Forest Edge Church in Sherwood Forest, for the marriage.

Friar Tuck stood at the altar and welcomed everyone. The guests of honor sitting at the front included Little John and Will Scarlet, Allan a Dale and his wife Ellen, Tim the Tanner, Midge the miller, Robert, the Sheriff's old cook and Tom Turnbull, the landlord of the Blue Boar Inn.

They all kept turning their heads to look back to the church door, waiting for Robin to arrive with Marian on his arm.

At last, the great door opened. The smiling figures of Robin and Marian walked slowly into the church. Robin was wearing a new tunic of Lincoln green. Marian wore a white cotton dress, made for her by Ellen. It was decorated with the brightest spring flowers. She also had a band of wildflowers around her head.

The happy couple reached the altar and knelt down. Friar Tuck blessed them before beginning the marriage ceremony.

Suddenly, there was a disturbance at the back of the church. The door crashed open and everyone turned towards it. Three men now stood in the doorway . . . Prince John, the

Three men now stood in the doorway.

Sheriff of Nottingham and Sir Guy of Gisborne.

The Sheriff made a signal and a small army of his soldiers, swords drawn, rushed past him into the church. "I want Robin and his men alive!" he shouted.

Such was the surprise of the attack that Robin's men and all the wedding guests were surrounded in moments. They didn't even have time to draw their weapons.

Robin, though, fought like a tiger, and it took a dozen men to eventually overpower him. Disarmed and with his hands tied behind his back, he was lashed to a pillar by the altar.

It wasn't until Robin was safely bound that the three villains entered the church.

"How nice to see you all," sneered the Sheriff as he walked slowly down the aisle with a look of triumph on his face.

Chapter 24
The Black Knight

The Sheriff approached Robin and poked him in the stomach with his sword.

"It seems your luck finally ran out," he said. "A little bird told me I might find you here. They said you had a wedding in mind. Funny that. I thought a hanging might be a better idea!"

"Hang me, by all means," replied Robin proudly. "But there will always be honest men in Sherwood Forest who will fight you to the end."

"Certainly not your Merry Men," laughed the Sheriff. "Every man here will end up on a rope before the sun sets this evening."

The Sheriff then turned to look at Little John. "And that includes you, Reynold Greenleaf! I believe that was the name you used when you robbed me blind while in my employ."

Little John laughed out aloud. "Ha!" he

The Black Knight

"It seems your luck finally ran out."

said, "your treasure has already been safely returned to the poor people you stole it from."

"Oh, I'm sure they will be quite happy to return it to me," said the Sheriff. "My men are probably knocking on their doors at this very minute."

The Sheriff turned and beckoned to Sir Guy to approach the altar. Then he grabbed Marian by the hand and pushed her into Sir Guy's arms.

"You may remember," said the Sheriff, turning back to look at Robin, "how you came to this church once before. Then you robbed Sir Guy of his bride, young Ellen. Well, I am about to rob you of your bride! And I think there will just be time to have a wedding before a hanging."

Now the Sheriff poked Friar Tuck with his sword. "My fat little Friar," he said, "there's work to do. Sir Guy would be most grateful if you would marry him to young Marian."

"Never!" shouted Friar Tuck.

"Oh, I don't think you can refuse," said the Sheriff, nodding to some of his men.

Four of the Sheriff's men approached the friar from behind and hauled him before Sir Guy and Marian, who was now in tears. With four swords aimed at his back, Friar Tuck had no choice. He began the wedding ceremony.

Robin strained with every ounce of his strength to free himself. It was hopeless. The ropes binding him to the pillar would have held ten men. The hated Sheriff seemed to have won the final battle.

Suddenly, the main church door crashed open. The Sheriff turned around, just in time to see a horse standing in the entrance. And on its back was a giant of a man, dressed from head to toe in black steel armor.

He pushed her into Sir Guy's arms.

157

"Seize that man!" shouted the Sheriff to his men.

Six soldiers, swords drawn, raced down the aisle and attacked the man, hacking at his armor. The Black Knight seemed unconcerned at the men attacking him. He swatted them down like flies with his own sword.

"Sheriff!" roared the Black Knight, riding a few steps up the aisle. "Order your men to put away their swords. The next soldier to draw his weapon will be a dead man."

"You can't kill all my men," snarled the Sheriff.

"I don't want to kill any of your men,' said the Knight. "My dear Sheriff, while you may be a traitor, I'm sure your men are as good as any proud Englishmen."

Then the strangest thing happened. First, two or three soldiers put down their weapons. Then others followed. Soon every one of the Sheriff's men had put aside their weapons.

The Black Knight hadn't used any special magic. But his words had been spoken with such authority that every soldier in the church immediately recognized that this stranger was no young stripling. He spoke as if he was used to being obeyed.

The Black Knight

The Sheriff screamed at his men to arm themselves again. But they were not to be swayed. Now each man edged away from the Sheriff, moving towards the Black Knight. It was as if they had decided to protect him rather than the Sheriff.

By this time Prince John was visibly trembling. He started to edge his way towards the door.

Suddenly, the Black Knight turned on him. "Prince John," he said, "I don't remember giving you permission to leave the church!"

The Prince made a final dash towards the door. But before he could open it, the Black Knight had reversed his horse and stopped him.

"What is your business here?" asked the Prince, who was now pinned between the horse and the door.

"I have come to stop some treacherous rebels stealing the Kingdom of England," the Black Knight replied.

Prince John caught his breath. He had not recognized the voice before, but he did now.

Chapter 25
Sir Robin of Sherwood Forest

"Good Knight," said Prince John, his knees beginning to shake. "Do I know you?"

"You know me well," answered the Knight.

"Give me your name!" snapped the Prince.

"Not yet," replied the Knight. "All I will say is that my armor may be black, but it is not nearly as black as your heart. Neither am I a man who would steal from his own people, as you and your henchmen do."

As he said the words, the Black Knight pointed to the Sheriff and Sir Guy of Gisborne.

"Good, sir," pleaded the Sheriff, who had no idea who the Knight might be. "What is your business here? You are welcome to join our wedding feast."

"Liar! This is no wedding feast!" bellowed the Black Knight, pointing first at Robin, still tied to the pillar, and then at Marian, at the altar with Sir Guy.

The Knight then spoke quietly to Marian.

"Is Sir Guy your chosen husband?"

"No, sire," answered Marian in a nervous voice.

"And would it be true," continued the Knight, pointing at Robin, "to say that young Robin Hood over there is the one you would marry."

"It is true," said Marian.

The Black Knight turned to the Sheriff. "If you value your life, you will free Robin Hood this minute."

"But he is an outlaw," protested the Sheriff. "He has stolen the King's deer. The punishment is death!"

"From what I hear," replied the Knight, "you are a bigger outlaw than Robin Hood. You'd steal the King's country if you could. Now free him immediately!"

"I shall not!" cried the Sheriff. "I am the law in Nottingham. I have my powers from the King himself. Robin Hood must hang!"

The Black Knight dismounted from his horse and walked slowly up the aisle. He stopped at the altar and turned around to face everyone in the church.

Then he removed his helmet.

The Sheriff dropped to his knees in shock.

Prince John looked as though he had seen a ghost.

It was Richard the Lionheart, King of England.

Gasps of surprise echoed around the church.

"Now will you free Robin?" asked the King.

The Sheriff scuttled across the floor and untied Robin's ropes.

The outlaw approached the King and dropped to his knees. "My Lord," he said, "we have long awaited your return. The country needs you."

The King smiled and shouted to one of the soldiers by the church door. "Bring in Sir William and his band of men!"

A few moments later Will Stutely came into the church with the men he had taken with him to Austria.

"Sir William?" asked a puzzled Robin.

The King explained that he had knighted Will for his bravery in rescuing him from the Duke of Austria. "Without the help of Will and his men, I might never have escaped from the Duke's castle."

Just then, Prince John made another move to escape from the church. He was almost

It was Richard the Lionheart, King of England.

through the door when a soldier put out a foot and sent him tumbling.

"You are my brother, but you are a cowardly knave," said the King. "You are so unlike Robin Hood. He is a king of outlaws, a prince of good men. I heard of his good deeds a thousand miles from England in the Holy Land . . . just as I heard of the villainy of you, the Sheriff and Sir Guy."

The King drew out his sword and touched Robin Hood on both shoulders with it. "Now arise, Sir Robin Hood."

Robin Hood had gone down on his knees as an outlaw. Now he rose as a Knight of England.

"You also have my royal pardon," continued the King, "for any of those deeds which this traitorous Sheriff of Nottingham would have hanged you for."

The King had a few more things to say to Robin. "I have made you a knight, but you have the choice of name you wish to take," he said. "You can choose whatever name you want, but I beg that you ride beside me for as long as I am king."

"If it pleases you, my lord, I shall be Sir Robin of Sherwood Forest," said Robin. "But I would ask for one more thing."

"And what is that, Sir Robin?"

Robin seemed almost afraid of what he wanted to say. "Some time ago," he said, "I told the Sheriff of Nottingham that I was my own man and wanted no man to be my master. It is still my wish to be my own master. I would rather be plain Robin, living with my sweet Marian in Sherwood Forest. A palace in London is not for me."

"By the good Lord, you are a bold fellow," smiled the King. "And anyone bold enough to deny me a favor deserves to have his wish granted. Sir Robin you are free to live your life as you wish."

The King had one more reward for Robin. "I shall take care of my brother's punishment. But I shall leave the Sheriff and Sir Guy in your hands. Will you have them hanged?"

"We must be merciful," said Robin. "I think it would be better if they were made to make amends for their evil."

Friar Tuck spoke up. "Well said, Robin. But we still have a marriage to perform between you and your lovely bride. I beg you that we do not do it here; every time I begin a marriage service in this church, the door bursts open and someone comes and points a sword at my head!"

166

"Now arise, Sir Robin Hood."

"Where would you like to perform the cere- mony?" asked Robin.

"Beneath the Great Oak in Sherwood Forest, of course!" smiled Friar Tuck.

Robin and Marian could think of no better place to get married.

Chapter 26
A Wedding in Sherwood Forest

The great day of Robin and Marian's wedding finally arrived. It was high summer and Sherwood Forest rang to the sound of happy laughter, and people busying themselves as they prepared for the marriage. The long table beneath the Great Oak had been extended to seat all the guests. A small altar had been built beside the oak tree.

That morning, the tracks through Sherwood Forest were busy with people traveling to the wedding. In the past, few would dare to enter the forest so openly. Now peace reigned in and around the ancient woodland.

"Is everything ready, old friend?" Robin asked Friar Tuck.

"It's as ready as it ever will be," answered the friar. "I just hope you can guarantee a peaceful wedding for a change."

"I promise you," said Robin, "that this wedding will go without any trouble at all."

"And what about the Sheriff of Nottingham?" asked Friar Tuck. "He won't be coming will he?"

"The Sheriff will be too busy to come," laughed Robin. "He has a new job. Remember how King Richard said that I must decide his future? Well, I thought long and hard, and finally decided on a perfect job for him."

"And what would that be?" asked the friar.

"He has been a burden to the people of Nottingham for many a year," explained Robin. "So now he is to feel that very same burden. He is to spend the rest of his life carrying people across the river beside Forest Edge Church."

The friar roared with laugher until his sides were sore. "A perfect job!" he spluttered. "And what of Sir Guy?"

"I've sent him to work for Midge, the miller and his father," replied Robin. "He will spend the rest of his life carrying great sacks of flour around to earn a fair living!"

That afternoon, all the guests gathered around the Great Oak. There were some familiar faces but unfamiliar titles.

There was Sir Will Scarlet, the new Sheriff of Nottingham. There was also Sir Little John, the new Chief Forester of Sherwood, and Allan a Dale, the King's new minstrel.

Soon after their arrival, the ringing of bridles was heard as Marian and her family arrived on horseback. She was wearing the same white dress she had worn at Forest Edge Church. Allan a Dale, playing on his lute, escorted her to the altar.

Poor Friar Tuck wondered if something was going wrong again when the sound of galloping horses was heard approaching.

The friar went down on his knees and looked to the heavens. "Not again, Lord," he pleaded, expecting to see the Sheriff and Sir Guy riding in.

He need not have worried. At that moment King Richard the Lionheart arrived in the clearing with a small group of soldiers. He had come for the wedding. The whole wedding party and the guests all bowed to their sovereign.

Soon after, Sir Robin of Sherwood and Lady Marian were married.

There never was a happier day in Sherwood Forest.

Allan a Dale escorted her to the altar.

Chapter 27

The Beginning of the Legend of Robin Hood

Robin and Marian lived a happy life together in Sherwood Forest. They had several children and built a fine home, right beside the Great Oak tree.

Most of Robin's men went away to join King Richard's army. But every year on midsummer's day, many of them returned to Sherwood to spend a few days with Robin and Marian. They talked long into the night about old times and old comrades.

In winter time, Sir Will Scarlet held a great banquet in Nottingham Castle for his old outlaw friends. In spring, Robin and his Merry Men always went to Forest Edge Church for a service of blessing.

Of course, the Sheriff of Nottingham carried them all across the river.

In time, all the Merry Men grew old. Each

A fine home, right beside the Great Oak tree.

year, fewer and fewer of them were able to visit Sherwood.

Robin eventually died and was buried at Kirklees Priory in Yorkshire.

But his death did not mark the end of his story. It was just the beginning.

It was only then that the legend of Robin Hood began to spread across England. The King's minstrels wandered the length and breadth of England, singing of the life of Robin Hood, his Merry Men, the Sheriff of Nottingham and Sherwood Forest.

Every man who heard the story repeated it to his own children. And, in turn, they told their children.

***

So over hundreds of years, the stories have finally reached you, the modern reader. Of course, they have changed over the years in their telling. Heroes have become even braver. No doubt, Little John has grown larger than ever. Friar Tuck has probably become fatter in the telling of the legend. Somehow, all stories become a little bigger and better with retelling.

Robin Hood

If you don't believe the stories, take a journey to Nottingham in England today; visit the castle where the Sheriff lived and walk the narrow streets where Robin once strolled.

But most of all, visit Sherwood Forest!

The forest is not as large as it used to be and it's not such a frightening place as it was in Robin's day.

Yet, wander through Sherwood on a warm summer's evening, just as the sun is setting. Look around you; feel the eyes watching you

Feel the eyes watching you.

176

from the thick greenwood; hear voices laughing and the ring of horses' bridles; smell the roasting venison on the blazing fire.

Robin Hood and his Merry Men were all real people, once upon a time. And today, their ghosts can still be heard singing and feasting around the crackling fire, beneath the Great Oak in Sherwood Forest.

The End